A TEST FOR TAYESHA

by Tara Demps Soyinka

FICTION

Published by
Just Us Books
356 Glenwood Ave.
East Orange, NJ 07017
www.justusbooks.com

Just Us Books, Inc.
356 Glenwood Avenue,
East Orange, NJ 07017

NEATE™ was created by Wade Hudson and is a trademark of Just Us Books, Inc.

Cover art copyright 2006 by Peter Ambush.

A TEST FOR TAYESHA

NEATE™ Book #5

ISBN:1-933491-01-9

Library of Congress Cataloging-in-Publication Data is available

First edition, Printed in Canada

10 9 8 7 6 5 4 3 2

To my mother, Mrs. Earline Demps Gilbert,
the wind beneath my wings.
—T.D.S.

A TEST FOR TAYESHA

NEATE ™ BOOK #5

* CHAPTER ONE *

"Tayesha! I hope you're awake and on your way downstairs." The gentle, but firm voice floated up the stairs to Tayesha's room. In her bed, Tayesha turned her head toward the door and yawned sleepily. She sat up, swung her feet over the side of the bed, and sat there, trying to gather enough strength to get up.

"I'm coming, Ma," Tayesha called. But instead of getting up, she flopped backward on the bed and looked lazily at the ceiling.

"Okay, girlfriend, get moving before Mama comes up to move you," Tayesha told herself. She stood up slowly and plodded barefoot across the plush carpet of her bedroom to the tiled floor of the hallway bathroom. The cool, smooth surface helped wake her up, and for this she was thankful. This was one morning that she needed all the help she could get.

Tayesha's stomach growled as she swept her hand across the bathroom wall to find the light switch. Instinctively, she shielded her eyes, and wondered why lights always seemed so much brighter after you just woke up. Her eyes finally adjusted, Tayesha brushed her teeth, showered and dressed, then made her way downstairs.

She was anxious to see what her mother made for breakfast, but midway down the steps Tayesha paused to look at the photos along the stairwell wall. The pictures had been up for years, but today she looked at them as if seeing them for the first time.

Memories washed over Tayesha as she gazed at the portraits. She smiled at the candid shot from her third birthday party. Her parents told her to put her face in the cake. Then they took a picture. Tayesha laughed at the white icing that adorned her young, pudgy face. Very funny, Mama and Daddy.

Her memories fast-forwarded. Winning the third grade spelling bee. Fifth grade graduation. Summer camp last year when she got poison ivy. Yuck!

"Tayesha Williams!" The clearly displeased voice of her mother called Tayesha back to the present.

"Coming!" Tayesha stalled.   She walked down the steps and spotted one of her favorite pictures of her parents on their wedding day. In the twenty-year-old portrait, the chocolate brown of her father's face contrasted with the alabaster of her mother's. Her dad's low Afro and her mom's short straight blond bob looked about as much alike as winter boots and summer sandals.

Tayesha pushed back a lock of her curly, sandy brown hair and touched her smooth golden skin.

"My dad's Black and my mom's White," Tayesha mused aloud as she gazed at the faces of the people she loved most in the world. "No problem for me. I just wish it weren't a problem for other people."

With that, she walked the rest of the way down the stairs to join her family for breakfast.

* * * * * * *

"Breakfast is delicious, hon," Mr. Williams declared as he wiped his mouth and placed his napkin on the table. "As always." He smiled at his wife who was sitting across from him. Greta Williams returned his smile.

They met twenty years ago when the then Army Private Harold Williams, fresh out of basic training in Illinois, was sent to Germany. He and Tayesha's mom caught each other's eye in a coffee shop and they had been together ever since. Greta Williams' parents hadn't been too happy when their only child brought home a six-foot three, African-American soldier. Only when Tayesha was born did they defrost. Tayesha only saw her mom's side of the family about once every few years due to the miles that separated them, and it was always a visit she eagerly anticipated.

Tayesha nodded her head enthusiastically in her mother's direction.

"Yes, Mama. These pancakes are slammin'!" she agreed. She dipped a sliver of pancake into a pool of maple syrup. She was sitting between her parents, the spot she had favored since she was a little girl.

Greta Williams nodded her head in acknowledgment of her family's praise.

"I thank you, sir and mademoiselle. I do my best."

Mrs. Williams turned to her daughter. "And speaking of doing one's best, it's Friday, and I remember that somebody has a big audition today!" She winked at her only child.

Dusable Junior High's drama department was holding auditions for an original play, "Downside Up Day." The play was about a girl named Ashley who wakes up one day to find that though she looks the same, she has become somebody else. The role of Ashley was a challenging one because the actor would have to play two different people. The actor would also have to convey the frustration Ashley feels in having her life dramatically altered, and in being forced to deal with the expectations other people have of her because they think she is someone else. Tayesha wanted the part of Ashley.

"Shoot," she had confided to Naimah, one of her best friends, "sometimes I feel like I'm two different people. Because of the way I look, people have expectations that usually don't go with who I am. That Ashley role has my name written all over it." Tayesha had laughed, but the smile didn't quite make it up to her eyes.

Tayesha could only nod at her mother because her mouth was full of pancakes.

"Yes, Mama. It's today," she said after she swallowed. She smiled wryly. "I know it's today because I feel like some butterflies and their cousins have moved into my stomach," she joked.

"You'd be surprised at how many well-known people get nervous before appearing in front of a group," Mr. Williams said.

"Butterflies are normal, baby girl. You just go on that stage, do your best and have fun. I know it took a lot of courage for you to decide to try out for this play. We're proud of you already, princess."

Tayesha smiled at her dad. "Thanks, Daddy. It's the waiting that's driving me crazy. I'll be glad when it's time for me to go on stage. Now I know how Liz feels when she's about to perform."

Elizabeth was another one of Tayesha's best friends and a member of NEATE, a closely-knit group of neighborhood friends. NEATE was the first initial of all of the friends' names: Naimah, Elizabeth, Anthony, Tayesha, and Eddie. Liz's dream was to be the next singing sensation. And she has what it takes, Tayesha thought proudly of her friend as she gulped down the rest of her breakfast. I just hope I do, too, she thought to herself.

"Going out for this play is going to be good for me, in more ways than one," Tayesha said to her parents. "Goodbye old scared, shy Tayesha," she whispered to herself. She couldn't wait until 3:30.

* CHAPTER TWO *

"Tayesha's on her way up, up in the world," Liz quipped in a reference to the play Tayesha would be auditioning for that afternoon. "Not the downside, but the *up*side."

"Ladies and gentlemen. Boys, girls, and squirrels all over this great big world!" Tayesha's friend Anthony took on the voice of an announcer as he "talked" into an invisible microphone.

"It's the lady of the hour! Here she is…Dusable Junior High's rising new actress and upcoming star of "Downside Up Day"…Tayesha Williams!" Anthony clapped in Tayesha's direction.

"Boys, girls, and squirrels?" Naimah shook her head as she put a straw into her juice carton. "You are so silly."

The five friends chatted together easily as they sat in the school's cafeteria, which had been given the name "The Corral" some years back. The wooden sign hung over the double doors just outside the

Many a joke had been made about the
students were served in the Western-
themed lunchroom.

"I am a bundle of nerves, y'all," Tayesha
admitted.

"Girlfriend, mark my words. You are going to
blow that audition up! You *are* Ashley."

"I was so happy and surprised when you said you
were trying out for the play," Liz said. "With your shy
self."

Tayesha smiled and looked over at Naimah.
Naimah grinned and gave Tayesha two thumbs
up. The level-headed, sensitive one of her friends,
Naimah guessed that Tayesha felt a connection with
the lead character before Tayesha even told her.

Tayesha turned away from Naimah and looked
out of the large cafeteria windows into the world
beyond. She was lost in thought about her upcoming
audition when she turned her head and noticed
Eddie looking at her. She raised her eyebrows to ask
"What's up?" Eddie turned away without responding.
Tayesha dismissed it, until she glanced at him again.
Eddie was looking at her, with a strange expression
on his face.

"Okay, Eddie. What's on my face? Ketchup?"
Tayesha laughed. The others glanced up to check.

Eddie looked at her sternly. "What are you talking about, Tayesha?"

Tayesha sucked her teeth. "As if you don't know. You're staring at me."

"What are you talking about, Tay?" Eddie asked her and shrugged.

Tayesha just looked at him. If Eddie wanted to play dumb, it was fine with her. She turned her attention to her lunch. She opened a pack of ketchup and squeezed out its contents, but her thoughts returned to Eddie. Tayesha was sure he was staring at her—hard too, like she had a message on her forehead. She dipped a French fry in a pool of red and swirled it around.

Naimah cleared her throat. "Now remember, as soon as the audition ends, you call us and tell us everything, okay?" she instructed.

Tayesha nodded. "Yes, ma'am," she joked. "The minute I get in the door."

Naimah looked at her watch. "Lunch is almost over, guys. The bell will be ringing before we know it."

Silence fell on the table as everyone ate. Except Tayesha. She really didn't have an appetite. Again she stared out of the large cafeteria windows into the courtyard. Now she was worried about stage fright.

Tayesha had a vivid image of herself standing on the stage being unable to speak. She shuddered at the thought.

When she rejoined the conversation at the table, Naimah was in the middle of a Rodney story. She was always keeping her friends entertained with stories of her eight-year-old brother. This time she was telling the group how Rodney's pet lizards had escaped from their terrarium and ended up in her favorite pair of sneakers.

"So the lizards have been banned from the house. They now live behind the house," Naimah emphasized, putting her hand behind her juice carton.

"It could have been worse," Liz remarked as she nibbled on an orange slice. "Rodney's pets could have been spiders."

"Yeah," Naimah agreed, shifting uncomfortably. "Yuck!"

Tayesha glanced at Eddie. He was staring straight ahead as he chewed his food almost mechanically. The lights were on but nobody seemed to be home. What was up with him today?

"Hey, Eddie. You haven't said a word in the last fifteen minutes." Totally weird, Tayesha thought.

"What am I supposed to say?" Eddie asked her.

Tayesha didn't look at him as she spoke. "I don't know. You're just too quiet."

"Yeah," Naimah added. "Maybe he's up to something," she said mischievously. The others grinned. "It's not like you to be quiet…"

"Will you just leave me alone?" Eddie snapped back. "Must I be harassed while I eat my food?" he asked, annoyed. He nudged Anthony. "Hey, man, be careful. The Don't Be Quiet While Eating Your Food Patrol is on the loose."

Tayesha, Naimah, Liz, and Anthony just looked at him. Tayesha couldn't believe how Eddie was acting. First the staring, now this. They were teasing him, but that's what they always did. And he was being quiet…

"Well, excuse us," Tayesha said, her feelings hurt.

"Sorry, Eddie," Naimah said as she dug out a forkful of strawberry shortcake. "You guys like your dessert?" she asked, changing the subject. "This is really good stuff for 'The Corral.'"

"What is everybody doing this weekend?" Liz asked. "Maybe we could hit the mall," she suggested. She loved shopping almost as much as she loved singing. "We could see a movie while we're there. I think a day just hanging out would be good for all us."

Anthony stuffed the last bite of sandwich into his mouth. "Yeah, Liz. We can celebrate Tayesha's going out for the play, no matter how it ends up. But I know you're going to get the role," he said to Tayesha. "You're going to do great."

Tayesha smiled her thanks.

Eddie's voice surprised her.

"Just don't forget us little people when you make it to the top," he said, pointing a lazy finger at Tayesha. She was surprised, but glad he'd decided to become part of the conversation so she played along.

"I'll never change, Eddie," Tayesha began. "I promise not to forget all of the people who assisted me in my climb to the top of the mountain of fame and fortune..." She put her hand over her heart dramatically and laughed. The others laughed with her, but when Tayesha looked at Eddie, there wasn't a trace of a smile on his mocha brown face. Tayesha frowned as she sampled another fry. Normally Eddie would have been talking nonstop and would have cracked about five jokes by now. Could he be trying to be more grown up? Tayesha mentally shook her head. Nah!

"Did she say, 'the top of the mountain of fame and fortune?'" Liz turned to Naimah incredulously. "This girl is truly tripping."

"Un-hunh," Naimah agreed. "She's changing and she hasn't set foot on a stage yet. What a shame."

"I'm the same person, I am!" Tayesha cried, melodramatically. "Why, I still take the bus to the mall!"

"Oh, boy. Get me an Oscar." Anthony pretended to gag. "Is the girl an actress or what?"

"Or what," Eddie said dryly.

He said it so softly, it might have been missed. But all four at the table heard Eddie and his ugly tone. Naimah dropped her fork in her strawberry shortcake. Liz stared open-mouthed at him. Tayesha's eyes were blinking like a yellow caution light.

"You know that was messed up, right?" Anthony said matter of factly.

Liz was angry. "You know Tay's sweating bullets about this audition today. How could you say something so thoughtless and rude?"

Eddie cooly slurped his juice.

"What? I'm kidding, okay?" Eddie shifted uncomfortably in his seat. His face was a mask of anger. "Isn't that what you all are used to? Joke-cracking Eddie? Well, there's a joke. Ha, ha, ha. Is that better? Jeez!"

"Eddie, you know better than to say something

like that, even in joking. We're all friends here. We're supposed to have each others' back." Naimah reminded.

"Ah, he's probably just stressed about that math test we've got this week," Anthony offered. "Let it go. This time," he added pointedly. Eddie rolled his eyes.

Math test my foot, Tayesha thought. As the others finished their lunch, Tayesha anxiously munched a single French fry in silence.

* CHAPTER THREE *

School was over for the day and Tayesha and Liz walked across the campus. Though classes had officially ended, plenty of other students were still milling around. Some were sitting and talking in clusters while others were waiting to be picked up. There were also those involved in extracurricular activities who would be on campus for several more hours. Tayesha belonged to the latter group.

As they walked, Liz gave Tayesha last-minute performing tips. Tayesha nooded her head as Liz instructed her on everything from acting naturally to voice control.

"Yes, yes," Tayesha answered. "Anything else, Mama?"

"Oh, Tayesha," Liz said, hugging her friend. "You're going to be great."

Tayesha grinned. "Thanks, Liz."

They turned to look at the Garvey M. Clarke Auditorium, which loomed before them.

Liz looked at her friend and squinted in thought.

"Gosh, Tay. I'm just thinking back to the first time I got on a stage and performed in front of an audience. I was four."

Tayesha was all ears. "Weren't you nervous? I've done speeches in church before, but never anything big like this."

Liz nodded understandingly. "I was all excited at first, but when I got on stage and saw those bright lights and all those people looking at me, I froze."

"For real?" Tayesha couldn't imagine Liz ever being scared on stage or anywhere else for that matter.

Liz nodded. "But then I saw my mom in the audience, mouthing the words to the song, and I just took off. But I'll never forget that day."

She looked at the expression on Tayesha's face and quickly added, "But you're going to do fine. How are you feeling, sister girl?" Liz asked.

"Nervous, but excited. I am ready to do this!" She put her hand on her hip playfully.

"Ooo-wee!" Liz whistled. "Well, check you out." Then she took on the stance of a coach. "How're you feeling!" she said loudly.

"Pumped up?" Tayesha balled her hands into fists.

"Say it like you mean it!"

"Pumped up!"

"Say it again."

"I said, I'm pumped up!"

"That's right. Now go get that part!"

* * * * * *

Tayesha entered the auditorium and was surprised to see so many students. There had to be at least eighty kids there, all waiting to audition. Tayesha wondered how many were trying out for the role of Ashley. She took a seat near the back and tapped her foot nervously. Maybe this was all a mistake. Why did she ever think she could audition for a major play and get the lead role? Tayesha had nearly talked herself into leaving when a smiling face appeared on the stage.

"Welcome, young people, to the drama department! For those of you who do not know me, I am Mrs. Kemp and this is my first year as the chorus and drama teacher here at Dusable Junior High. Thank you for coming to audition for our upcoming play, 'Downside Up Day.'"

Mrs. Kemp was a petite woman in her early thirties. She looked out at the students in the audience as she spoke to them from the stage. "I hope you have all familiarized yourselves with the plot of the play. We are looking for expression and truth." She smiled again as she surveyed the crowd.

"I see a lot of faces I've never seen before. How many of you have never taken a drama class?" Tayesha raised her hand. Dozens of other hands joined hers. Mrs. Kemp clapped her own hands together.

"Wonderful! I am pleased to see so many new actors in the house. Please, please, just be natural when you audition. Do not feel it's necessary to sound like you are acting. Acting is about being, about feeling and responding as the character truly would."

Mrs. Kemp took a deep breath and continued.

"I, along with two of your peers, will decide who will return for this Monday's callback. Just as the name implies, a callback is when someone trying out for a part is asked to return and read again. It's our second and final round of auditions. We'll use the callbacks to make our final selections for the cast."

Two girls walked out onto the stage to join Mrs. Kemp.

"These are the students who will be helping

judge the auditions," Mrs. Kemp explained. Tayesha had seen both girls around school but she didn't know their names.

"This is Brett Mulligan and this is Kaylie O'Donnell," Mrs. Kemp introduced the girls. "Please give them a hand." The auditioners applauded the two girls. Brett and Kaylie smiled confidently.

"Now, we'll begin the auditions," Mrs. Kemp said. "Good luck to all of you."

"Number one," Brett called. Tayesha watched as a boy walked uncertainly to the stage. Each student auditioning had been given a number. Tayesha was number 35. She settled in to wait.

"What part are you going for, Tayesha?" a voice asked.

Tayesha turned and saw a familiar face. Michelle Davis sat two rows behind her in Algebra class.

"Oh, hey, Michelle. I didn't see you when I sat down," Tayesha said. "I'm trying out for the part of Ashley. What about you?"

"It doesn't matter. I just want to be in the play." Michelle looked around the auditorium. "We have a lot of competition. You nervous?"

Tayesha nodded. "Yeah," she admitted. "You?"

"Oh, yeah. If they don't call my name soon, I may

walk out of here!" Michelle said. Tayesha laughed. She was glad to have Michelle to talk to while she waited for her name to be called. It made time pass quickly.

"Number 25," Kaylie called.

Michelle stood up. "That's my number," she whispered excitedly. "Well, good luck, Tayesha."

"Thanks. Good luck to you too," Tayesha whispered back.

Michelle approached the stage and began reading. It was obvious that she was nervous at first, but once she became comfortable on stage, she was good. She was auditioning for the part of Ashley's best friend, Whitney. Tayesha thought it would be really cool if she won the part of Ashley and Michelle won the part of Whitney. Before Tayesha knew it, Michelle's audition was over. Her friend exited the stage to polite applause. Tayesha clapped and shifted in the hard seat as she watched other students audition. When would Mrs. Kemp call her number?

"Number 35," Kaylie called.

Tayesha's number was up. She took a deep breath and walked onto the stage.

"Ashley has just awakened to find that she is someone else," said Mrs. Kemp. "You may begin reading."

Tayesha felt the butterflies from breakfast return in a serious way. She looked out into the dimmed theater and took a deep breath. "You are Ashley," she told herself. Reading the script, Tayesha got in the bed on stage and pretended to be asleep. Another girl she didn't know was auditioning for the part of Ashley's mother. The girl knocked on the prop door, and called, "Ashley, honey. Wake up. You'll be late for school." Tayesha smiled a little. Was this a scene from her real life or what? She yawned and stretched in bed.

"I'm coming, Mom." Tayesha got out of bed and walked sleepily across the floor just as she did at home. It didn't even feel like acting!

"Boy," Tayesha said, scratching her head as she walked across the floor. "I feel really weird. I hope I'm not catching a cold." She walked downstage past an imaginary bedroom mirror. She stopped abruptly and walked slowly back to peek into the "mirror". A look of confusion crossed her face, and then dismay. With all of her being, Tayesha yelled, "MOM!" Then she fell to the stage floor.

The audience erupted with applause. As she pulled herself up, Tayesha glanced at Mrs. Kemp and the student judges, Brett and Kaylie. They were standing at opposite ends of the stage, smiling broadly and clapping along with the others.

Tayesha exited the stage and passed by Brett and Kaylie. They watched her as she approached.

Brett and Kaylie looked as if they belonged together. Both wore khaki bottoms, white tank tops and dark jean shirts. Even their shoulder-length blond hair was worn in a similar style.

"Oooh, you did great!" Brett gushed. "You are going to be a hard act to follow."

Tayesha smiled easily. "Thanks a lot."

"For sure," Kaylie concurred. "The other kids auditioning for Ashley are really going to have to work hard."

"I don't know about that," Tayesha said truthfully. "I just went out there and did my best."

"So, are you auditioning for any other roles besides Ashley?" Brett wanted to know.

It wasn't hard to see who the leader of the two student judges was. Brett was obviously used to calling the shots.

"Just curious," Kaylie added.

"I only want to be Ashley. That's why I tried out for it," Tayesha said.

"Well, everyone can't always get the roles they want," Brett said. Her voice was flat and her smile was gone. Tayesha looked at Brett, surprised. But within seconds, Brett was smiling again and Tayesha wondered if she'd heard Brett say what she thought she'd said. Kaylie was smiling too.

"Uh, I've gotta go," Tayesha said. "See you guys around."

"See you later," Brett called after her.

Tayesha stuck her thumbs in the loops of her jeans and went back out into the audience to watch the rest of the auditions. As she watched other students who were auditioning for the role of Ashley deliver some of the same lines she had just uttered, Tayesha couldn't help feel pleased with herself. She knew she had captured the lead character's panic, fear and confusion. Excited, she settled into the hard, wooden auditorium chair.

"Girl, you were good!" Michelle had hung around afterwards too.

"Thanks, Michelle," Tayesha said modestly.

Michelle looked earnest. "Who would have believed you had all that talent in shy you? Bet you'll get a callback."

Tayesha could only hope. "I hope so, girl. I hope we both get callbacks. It'd be fun working on the play together."

Michelle nodded. "Yeah, it would. Well, I'd better go. I told my parents I'd come straight home," she said. "I'll see you in class tomorrow."

Tayesha waved as Michelle walked down the aisle and out the side door of the auditorium. Tayesha's parents were right. Auditioning for the play was a good idea. It gave her a boost in confidence. Tayesha beamed and clenched her fists excitedly. She couldn't wait until Monday.

* CHAPTER FOUR *

Eddie walked into the house Friday after school, went straight to his room, and closed the door. He dropped his backpack in the spot where he was standing. It landed with a thud amidst all the other items that littered his floor. Kicking off his sneakers, he fell backward on his unmade bed and exhaled noisily through his nose. This was terrible! How did he get himself in such a fix? The worst thing about this problem was he couldn't tell anybody about it, especially his NEATE friends. This time, he was on his own.

Eddie put on his earphones, pushed "play" and stared at the ceiling. His portable CD player blaring in his ears, Eddie didn't hear the knock at his door.

"Eddie?" It was his mother. Juanita Delaney had heard her son come in, but he hadn't sought her out to greet her or talk about his day. She hadn't even heard the refrigerator door open. She knew something was wrong.

Mrs. Delaney knocked harder. The door was

unlocked, but she and Mr. Delaney tried to respect Eddie's privacy. They always knocked and waited for their son to answer. But if he didn't open the door in a reasonable amount of time, neither parent had a problem opening the door for him.

Knock, knock, knock!

"Martin Edward Delaney!"

Eddie finally heard her. He quickly got up and opened the door. His mom looked puzzled.

"Sorry, Mom," he smiled sheepishly. "I had on my earphones."

Mrs. Delaney pursed her lips, walked past her son and tried not to comment on what she saw before her. Chaos ruled the room. She looked around and saw the unmade bed, the discarded book bag parked in the middle of the floor, and the clothes, dirty and clean, at her feet. Her eyes rested on a pair of socks hanging pitifully over the headboard of Eddie's bed.

Juanita Delaney tilted her head questioningly, and then looked at her only son. The room could wait—for now.

"I didn't hear a 'Hey, Ma' when you came in," she smiled. "How was your day?"

Eddie nodded neutrally. "Alright, I guess."

His mother looked at him. "Are you okay, Eddie?"

Eddie nodded again and put on what he hoped was a convincing smile. "I'm fine, Ma. I just have a lot on my mind." Did he ever! But he didn't want his mother to know how worried he was. What he needed was some time to sort things out.

Mrs. Delaney didn't believe Eddie when he said he was fine, but she wanted to give him time. She always preferred that he come to her when he was ready to talk. Her eyes took in her son's room for a second time.

"Humph. You sure have a lot of cleaning to do in this hurricane of a room."

Eddie chuckled in spite of himself. "Yes, Ma." He plopped down on a not-so-cluttered space of his bed.

"Eddie?"

"Yeah, Ma?"

"You know that you can talk to me and your dad if something's on your mind. No matter what it is, right?"

"I'll second that!" Mr. Delaney stuck his head in his son's door and grinned. "What's up?"

"Nothing, Dad. You're home early!" Eddie was clearly excited to see his Dad.

Floyd Delaney returned his enthusiasm. "What's going on, son?" He walked in the room, over to his only son, and palmed his head with one hand.

"Ow! Don't hate me because I can ball and I've got brains." Eddie grabbed his basketball and spun it on his index finger.

"Oh, ho, ho! I'm impressed. And just where do you think you got both from? Especially the brains." Mr. Delaney blew on his knuckles and brushed them back and forth across his chest exaggeratedly.

Eddie shook his head like he was confused and grinned wickedly. "Unnn-unnh. That's a hard one."

"Oh, that's a hard one, huh? How about no allowance this week?" He threw two pillows at Eddie and Eddie doubled up with laughter.

The scene was a happy one. Eddie sighed and reflected on how far he and his dad had come. Until a little while ago, the two had been barely speaking to each other. With his less than stellar grades, and easy-going, playful attitude, Eddie doubted that he would ever live up to his father's high expectations and serious sense of responsibility. But after some help from his friends, some extra studying on Eddie's part, and more listening on his father's part, father and son had come to understand each other. Now their relationship was solid. Eddie smiled. Then, the remembrance of his problem hit him like a ton of bricks. Lately, his life had been one crisis after another.

Floyd Delaney noticed the look on his son's face and sat down next to him. He pulled a t-shirt from under a pile of books on Eddie's bed.

"Do you need to talk to us about something? Or to me?"

"No, sir. I'm cool." Eddie nodded nonchalantly. "Really, I'm cool." Eddie massaged his knuckles as he stared at the floor.

His parents exchanged glances then walked out of the room, his mother gently closing the door behind her. Though Eddie wouldn't admit it to them, his parents' support made him feel a little better. But his dilemma weighed on his mind like a pair of dumbbells.

"I'm going to have to keep this to myself. It would mess up everything if the others found out." Eddie sighed to himself as he began on his homework. "So they won't."

* CHAPTER FIVE *

As she'd promised, Tayesha sat down to call her friends as soon as she got home from the audition. She picked up the receiver and began dialing numbers she'd known by heart for years. She called Liz first. Busy. It figured. Liz was always on the phone. Tayesha called Naimah. Naimah squealed and told her friend that she was bound to get the role of Ashley. When Tayesha called Anthony, he went on about her certain future in show business. Her friends' enthusiasm gave Tayesha a warm feeling inside. Then she called Eddie. He answered on the first ring.

"What's up, Eddie?" she greeted him cheerfully.

"Nothin' much, Tayesha. What's up with you?"

"Nothin' much."

Silence.

"Were you busy?" she asked.

"Uh, a little." There was a pause. "Listen, I gotta go."

"You have to go?" Tayesha was in disbelief.

"Yeah." Eddie sounded impatient. "Listen, I'll talk to you later, alright?"

"But, Eddie..."

The dial tone stuttered and Tayesha was left dumbfounded, holding the phone.

* * * * * *

On Monday after school, Tayesha stood in the auditorium with the other acting hopefuls and scanned the callback list. Her anxious eyes found her name at the bottom of the list.

"Yeah!" she exclaimed. "I got a callback! Go, Tay, it's your birthday." She did a little dance—one step to the left, one step to the right, then a sashay around in a circle. Tayesha knew her parents and her friends would share her happiness. She ran to get Liz and Naimah and wordlessly showed them her name on the list.

"Oh, look out! That's great!" Liz hugged Tayesha. "Those judges have good taste."

"Aw, please. Thanks, Liz." Tayesha smiled at her girl's loyalty. Unlike ole ugly-acting Eddie Delaney. Weird to the "nth power." She told Naimah and Liz about her non-conversation with Eddie the day before.

Naimah tried to put it in perspective.

"I don't know, Tay, maybe..." Naimah searched for the right words, "maybe, you're just a little extra sensitive right now because you're all wrapped up in the excitement of the play," Naimah said. "I mean, he was a little snappy that day at lunch, but other than that..."

"It's normal though," Liz offered when she noticed the hurt in Tayesha's silence. "When I'm preparing for a talent show, I get kind of off-balanced. All I can think about is that one thing."

"Thanks," mumbled Tayesha as she bit her bottom lip. Naimah and Liz were trying to make Tayesha feel better, brushing off her concern about Eddie. But even as gentle as their words were, they only managed to make her feel worse. Tayesha thought back on the past couple of days. The faces of her best friends, Naimah, Anthony, Liz, and Eddie, flashed through her mind. Maybe Liz was right. Maybe she was obsessing over the play. Maybe all of her friends were tired of hearing about it, but Eddie was the only one who showed it. She wondered if she should stop talking about the play altogether. She couldn't afford to lose her friends over a play.

"You got a callback." Naimah's words snapped Tayesha out of her daze. "So what happens next?"

"You get a callback when the judges or casting people or whoever, want to get another look at you," Tayesha explained. "If I wow them at the callback, hopefully, I'll be chosen for the role of Ashley." Tayesha tried to stifle the excitement that was building, but her feelings won the battle.

"Oooh, I'm so excited, ya'll," she squealed. She glanced around the large room for Michelle but didn't see her. Tayesha went back to the list and scanned it for Michelle's name. She was disappointed to see that Michelle's name was missing from the list.

"We have reason to celebrate," Naimah said. "How about…today?" she looked hopefully at Tayesha.

"Okay," Tayesha agreed slowly. "How about we eat at…"

"Papa's Grill?" Liz and Naimah answered together. Papa's Grill was NEATE's favorite restaurant.

"It's already been decided," Naimah said. "We knew you would get a callback so the four of us decided to do this yesterday."

"Aw, guys…"

"Congratulations, Tay." Anthony walked up behind her.

"Hey, Anthony. Thanks. How long have you been standing there?" Tayesha asked.

"Long enough to know that you got the callback!" He gave her a hug. "Alright! I knew you'd get it."

Tayesha was ecstatic. "So Papa's Grill it is then. Celebration time!" she sang. "Wait guys. Let me use the restroom first," she told the group. "Don't leave without me."

"Of course," Liz said smiling. "You're the guest of honor."

Tayesha nodded as she half walked, half jogged to the girls' lavatory.

She used the bathroom and was buckling her belt in the stall when she heard low voices at the far end of the bathroom. She didn't pay much attention at first, but soon the conversation caught her ear.

"It made me literally sick to have to put her name on the callback list. Ugh! Can you believe her? 'I tried out for Ashley because it's the role I want.' Who does she think she is? She should be glad to get any role," said voice number one.

A second voice responded with a question. "What

is she, anyway?"

Tayesha had heard those voices before. They belonged to Brett and Kaylie, the student judges. Their question was one she had heard before too. And it didn't take a rocket scientist to know they were talking about her. Tayesha slowly stepped up on the lidless toilet seat, and prayed that she didn't fall in as she balanced on the inverted U. She dared not breathe too hard, or the other two girls might realize they weren't alone in the bathroom. And Tayesha wanted them to think they were.

"I think she's mixed, or biracial if you want to use the politically correct term. She thinks she's hot stuff because she did okay in the auditions," Brett said. Tayesha would know that haughty voice anywhere.

"Just okay? Come on, Brett," Kaylie responded. "She was the best of all the girls trying out for Ashley and you know it. She's the only Black girl in the running for the lead role, not that many tried out for Ashley or any other roles. There was that girl Michelle somebody, and," Kaylie lowered her voice to a whisper. "Hey, maybe we'd better talk over the phone. Someone could be in here with us."

"Nobody's in here, scaredy-cat, but us, some crusty sinks and toilets," Brett answered. She sucked her teeth. "Just to put your mind at ease, I'll show you."

Tayesha was horrified. They were going to check the stalls! She steadied her balance on her toilet perch. She could hear the girls doing what she guessed was a sweep for feet and legs under the stalls.

"See? Nothing," said Brett. Tayesha relaxed some. She figured the girls had finished talking about her. They weren't.

"Is biracial the same thing as Black?"

"Yeah, to me it is. And I don't want to pick any Black person for the lead role in our school play. That girl Michelle is in my Spanish class. She's nice, but "Annnk!" Brett imitated a buzzer. "Wrong color! And she was too nervous."

Brett turned into a game show announcer. "Michelle, you get the consolation prize. We'll pay you...no attention! Ha, ha, ha." Brett laughed at her own joke. Kaylie was silent. Brett continued.

"Maybe I'll give Tayesha a small part, but she ain't gonna get the starring role, baby! I don't care how spectacular she is, she will not play Ashley." A makeup compact creaked open.

"I hear you Brett, and, I'm, um, not crazy about the Black thing either, but, how are we not going to pick her? You heard Mrs. Kemp going on and on about how good she was. She was the reason Tayesha got the callback. It's going to be hard getting around Mrs. Kemp when we pick the final cast."

"Well, getting around Mrs. Kemp is just what we're gonna have to do, Kay." Brett's voice was cold and determined. "This is not going to be some hip-hop play with people rapping and dancing. This is theater," Brett emphasized in her best British accent.

"And we don't want one of *them* as our play's leading lady." Brett said with a toss of her head. "Just think about the Black people you know," Brett continued.

"I don't know, Brett," Kaylie began. "The only Blacks I know are the ones in our classes and I don't know them, know them. You know, like, hang out with them."

"Here's a newsflash, Kay. I don't hang out with them either. But hey, my parents know Black people. They work with them. And anybody who watches television, movies, or reads magazines knows what they're like," Brett said confidently. "That Tayesha girl is biracial which is Black, but worse!" she said emphatically. "Black people are supposed to be, well, black. But since she's light skinned, she thinks she can be with White people too." Brett snickered.

Tayesha was astonished. Who would believe all this? She certainly wouldn't if she had not heard it with her own ears. She pushed her fist to her open mouth. She felt like screaming and dunking those ignorant girls' heads in the toilet. Especially Brett. But Tayesha repositioned herself on the toilet instead.

Kaylie spoke next. "Brett. Don't you think you're just a little over the top about all this? I mean, you sound like you really hate Black people," Kaylie said quietly.

"I sound like I hate Black people?" Brett was obviously upset and was now yelling. Tayesha was glad because she no longer had to strain to hear their conversation.

"I can't believe you, Kaylie. Have you forgotten what that Black girl did to me last year?" Brett spat the words out.

"You were there at Lolly Land for the seventh grade trip. How would you feel if you got pushed into a fountain in front of everybody? Everybody laughed at me, Kay. Even the goofy, giant lollipop character was pointing and laughing! People still tease me about it. My parents were even considering having me change schools." Brett shook her head at the memory.

"I should have punched that girl in her big, laughing mouth and wrung her scrawny little neck." Brett paused and whispered angrily. "Whose side are you on?"

"Yours," Kaylie blurted out. "Ours, Brett. You know that."

"So what's up with the goody-two-shoes act then? 'Aren't you a little over the top about this, Brett?' " Brett mimicked. "We need to be together on this. I don't care how good that Tayesha girl is, she will not be Ashley."

Kaylie sighed. "I hear you, but remember that Mrs. Kemp has the final say. All we do is make recommendations."

"I know that. But what we have to do is convince Mrs. Kemp that someone else would be better for the role," she said excitedly. "Someone not biracial, Black, or whatever."

Kaylie was slow to respond. "We could get in a lot of trouble if someone finds out about what we're trying to do. I don't know, Brett… "

"What don't you know?" Brett snapped. "God, you can be such a baby. You know as well as I do that the role of Ashley was not written for a Black girl. Let the biracial actress star in a Black play. I hear they're bringing 'The Jeffersons' to the stage," Brett joked. "She could play Florence."

Kaylie couldn't help but giggle. "The Jeffersons," she repeated. "Now that was funny."

"That's why I like you, Kaylie. You know funny, and you have such good taste in friends." Brett said approvingly. "But anyhow. The Lolly Land thing wasn't the only run-in I had with a Black person, either. You remember that Black guy who told Ms. Niles I was cheating on last year's Pre-Algebra final?"

"You *were* cheating, Brett."

"That's beside the point," the girl huffed. "Tattletale jerk." A compact clicked closed.

"So picking that Tayesha girl for the lead is completely out of the question, agreed?"

"Alright," Kaylie said slowly.

"We'll just pick one of the other girls on the callback list and coach her so she'll be fantastic at the second audition." Brett enthused.

"I'm not saying that Black people can't be in the play, just not in a major role. Only a White person for the lead role." Brett added. "Nothing personal against

Tayesha or Black people, of course."

Finally, Tayesha heard shoes thud across the floor and the door swing close. Several seconds later she emerged from the bathroom stall, stiff and dazed.

"Nothing personal," she half-muttered and half-laughed.

The bathroom walls amplified her words and her hurt. They had smiled in her face and complimented her performance. And here they were talking about her behind her back.

Everyone can't always get the roles they want.

Tayesha remembered what Brett said to her after the auditions. She had slipped that into the conversation right after telling Tayesha how great her performance was. Tayesha couldn't believe Brett and Kaylie were plotting against her—how determined they were to keep her out of the lead role because of her race. Tayesha wondered, had everything been fair, would Michelle have gotten a callback too?

Tayesha knew she had to expose those girls, but how? She leaned against a sink and considered her options.

"If I tell Mrs. Kemp, it'll be my word against theirs," she thought aloud. "I've got to get proof somehow."

Tayesha plopped down on the cold tile floor. Hot, angry tears filled her eyes. She chided herself for crying, but she couldn't help it. This was so wrong. She had to prevent Brett and Kaylie from sabotaging her, but she had no idea where to start.

Grandma Williams, her dad's mother, often talked about being tested in life. She said, "It's just God's way of making you see what you are made of deep inside."

Tayesha rose and got tissue for her runny nose.

Black people are supposed to be black.

As much as she hated Brett for voicing it, she had to face the question that had been at the back of her mind for years. A question that she couldn't answer.

"With my too-light skin, and curly hair, am I really Black?" Tayesha whispered.

There was no answer for her, just the sounds from people in the hall passing by.

She stood up and faced herself in the mirror.

"I'm going to stand up to those girls and stop their wicked little plan," she said with a sureness that surprised her.

But how?

* CHAPTER SIX *

"Oooh. That's my song, guys! 'Dream a Little Dream,'" Liz exclaimed as she, Naimah, Anthony, and Tayesha walked past a car playing the classic tune. The four friends had left school and were on their way to Papa's Grill, which was about twenty minutes from campus.

Liz snapped her fingers to the beat and hummed. "I hope I'll hear myself on the radio one day," she said wistfully to no one in particular. It was a beautiful, spring day and the friends were laughing and talking as they walked. But Tayesha was miles away lost in thought.

The group turned into the restaurant's parking lot. Inside Liz spotted a table by a window. "Let's sit over there," Liz called out.

Regulars at Papa's Grill, the four friends ordered quickly without a menu, and talked as they waited for their food. Hanging out with her friends never failed to lift Tayesha's spirits whenever she was down. She was feeling a little better already.

"Now this is a sandwich!" Anthony proclaimed when their food arrived. "But I'll save extra room in case you all can't handle your large-sized portions." He took a bite. "Ummm-mmm! I'm gonna do this sandwich right! Like mom always says, 'Never let good food go to waste.'"

Tayesha made a face at him. "And you don't." She sampled her fried fish and the restaurant's signature spicy fries. Papa Patterson had outdone himself again. Tayesha looked around the restaurant to see if she could get a glimpse of the elderly chef. Naimah lightly tapped her fork against her water glass to get everyone's attention.

"Ahem," she said, beaming. "The purpose of this get together is to celebrate our girl, Tayesha, getting a callback for the role of Ashley in Dusable Junior High's play, 'Downside Up Day.'" Naimah and Liz whooped it up as everyone at the table applauded. Liz pointed at Tayesha.

"See that girl there? That girl can act! Gonna be a movie star." The others laughed.

Tayesha smiled shyly. "No, girl. You're the one who's going to be the star, with that voice you have."

The rest of the afternoon passed quickly. Tayesha tried to enjoy herself, but her thoughts kept returning to Brett and Kaylie and their little scheme. She and Michelle, the only two Black students who were trying out, might get recommended for supporting characters, but definitely not for the lead roles. Tayesha remembered seeing other students of color trying out for various parts: Maggie Le, Ngoc Kim, and Marisol Ramirez. She guessed they did not fit into Brett and Kaylie's vision either. The little witches.

"Hey, everybody." Naimah was looking at the restaurant's front entrance. "Eddie knew to meet us here at four. It's four thirty."

"He's probably got something on his mind," Anthony said. "He'll tell us eventually."

"Guys, I'm going to need your help with something," Tayesha said slowly.

"You know you can count on us. What's the problem?" Naimah placed her elbows on the table and rested her face in the palms of her hands.

Tayesha began. "You know it took me a long time in the bathroom?" Anthony, Liz, and Naimah nodded. "Well," Tayesha went on, "I was in the stall when the two girls who're helping to judge the auditions came in…." Her pulse quickened as she went on to describe what she had overheard in the bathroom. Her anger came back, but at the same time, telling her friends made her feel better. Tayesha knew her friends. And Brett and Kaylie didn't stand a chance at being successful with their scheme if NEATE had anything to do with it.

When Tayesha was finished talking, Anthony, Liz, and Naimah's mouths were wide open.

"I know those girls," Liz began. "Remember, guys, that girl Brett got pushed in the pool at Lolly Land last year." The others snickered in remembrance.

"Now we know why," Naimah said wryly.

"I even felt sorry for her when she got pushed into the water in front of everyone," Liz said. "Brett seemed okay. Maybe a little pushy …" Liz trailed off.

"Kaylie seemed nice too. She's in my fourth period English honors class. She's always asking me to give her my notes."

Anthony was livid. "Brett just asked me if I would tutor her! So they've got a problem with us, huh?" he said, rubbing his chocolate brown skin for emphasis.

"I get it." Naimah straightened her back. "Black people are good enough to give her notes and to tutor her, but not good enough for fun things, like the play," she said cynically. "It looks like we've got some work to do, guys."

Anthony nodded in her direction and leaned in.

His three friends shifted their empty plates to make room and leaned in as well.

"You'd better believe we do," Anthony confirmed. "We've got to expose these girls. How? I don't know right now, but exposure is the way to go. Confronting them about it is out of the question. All they'll do is deny it. So don't let on that you heard them today, Tay."

Tayesha nodded. "I won't."

"We're going to have to make sure everyone knows their criteria," he paused and lifted his fingers to make quotation marks in the air, "for judging the auditions." Anthony tapped his fingers against the Formica tabletop. "Maybe then, you and everybody will get a fair second audition. Let's meet Wednesday after school and brainstorm a plan."

"Sounds cool, Anthony," Tayesha said with a hint of sadness. She felt so lucky to have her friends. But she'd bothered them enough about the play already, and here she was bringing them closer to it.

"Hey, look, guys. It's Eddie," Anthony announced, putting up his finger to get Eddie's attention.

Eddie spotted Anthony and made his way over to the table, grinning. Tayesha looked at him as he walked toward them. Liz and Naimah scooted over to make room.

Eddie sat down, took off his baseball cap and put it on his left knee. "I didn't know if you guys would still be here. I see everybody's eaten already. What's up, ya'll?"

"Not much, Eddie. We didn't think you were coming, man," Anthony told him. "I told you four o'clock, remember?"

"Sorry. I had to talk to my science teacher about a project," Eddie said, looking around the table.

"Hey, Eddie. You're just in time." Naimah said. "We have a situation that needs to be dealt with, ASAP."

Eddie grunted. "What's the problem?"

"It has to do with Tayesha and the play," Liz said simply. "Go on and tell him, Tay. Eddie, no way are you going to believe this."

Before Tayesha could respond, Eddie shook his head in disbelief.

"It's always something with you, Tay. What is it this time?" He looked around the table like a comedian trying to connect with his audience. He paused, preparing to deliver the punch line of a joke. "Did somebody chase you home or something?"

Tayesha stiffened as she remembered the incident.

Hey, lemon! Is your mama White or something?

In her mind's eye, she flashed back to one of the most painful times in her thirteen-year-old life.

She had been walking to her grandmother's house, minding her own business, when several African-American boys began teasing and chasing her.

"Are you an Oreo? You sure look mixed up to me!"

"Are you White or are you Black?"

Tayesha squeezed her eyes closed and winced. Months later, it still felt like it had just happened yesterday.

Tayesha turned to Eddie and looked at him with hurt in her eyes. "How…could you…say…that to…me?" she asked. Four pairs of eyes were on Eddie, awaiting his answer. Nobody dared look at Tayesha.

The five friends grew up together on Mary Street and had been friends for as long as any of them could remember. They went to school together, laughed together, and helped each other. There had never been a major conflict between them. Until now.

Eddie realized the harm in his words too late.

"Hey, Tay," he said softly. "I…I…didn't mean

anything by it. Really I didn't. You know me."

Tayesha could not remember being so embarrassed and hurt by someone who was supposed to be a friend. Eddie had to know how deeply those words would cut. He knew about those boys, those boys who had taunted her because of her mixed heritage. She had told all four of her friends in confidence, knowing that she could trust them with her secret. Those boys were strangers. She could expect that from stupid strangers. But not from a friend. Make that a former friend. Tayesha blinked away tears of hurt and anger.

Naimah said softly, "We all need to talk." But no one heard her, least of all Tayesha. Tayesha looked at Eddie, her eyes filled with tears she refused to shed. She understood if he were annoyed because she talked about the play a lot, but to say what he said was uncalled for. And mean. She put money for her portion of the bill on the table.

"No, I don't know you, Eddie Delaney. And I don't think I ever did. I'll talk to you guys later."

Eddie, Anthony, Liz, and Naimah watched, not knowing what to say as Tayesha walked out of the restaurant and into the early spring chill.

* CHAPTER SEVEN *

"Tayesha, it's Eddie," Harold Williams called upstairs.

"I'm still busy, Daddy."

Tayesha sighed as she lay across her bed on her stomach. It was the third time Eddie had called that evening. Tayesha didn't want to talk to him. In fact, she didn't want anything to do with him. Minutes later, her father was standing in her doorway.

"May I come in, Tay?" Mr. Williams asked.

Tayesha nodded, and her father walked in and stood by her bed, looking down at her. Tayesha remained on her stomach, staring down at the floor.

"Tell me, why are you so upset with Eddie, Tay? I thought he was your friend."

"I thought so too, Dad," she said sadly. Tayesha sat up in her bed, cross-legged. She could feel a headache coming on. She rubbed her temples with her index fingers and she told her father how Eddie had been acting and what had happened in the restaurant. Her life had been turned upside down since she decided to try out for "Downside Up Day." Talk about irony, she thought grimly. But it was Brett's statement echoing in her mind, that really weighed heavily on her.

Black people should be black.

Tayesha silently remembered a time not so long ago, when she used tanning lotion and changed her hair so her racial heritage would be more obvious. Those actions seemed silly to her now, but the mindset behind them hadn't changed that much. Tayesha exhaled then looked seriously at her dad.

"Daddy, I have something to ask you. Do you think I'm Black enough?"

"What?" Harold Williams asked surprised. He sat back to get a better look at his daughter. "You've really had some heavy stuff on your mind, haven't you, young lady? 'Are you Black enough?' What would make you ask that, Tay?"

"Daddy, look at me. I'm very light-skinned and my hair is light brown. I don't look Black, do I?"

Harold Williams reached out for his daughter. Tayesha let her father hold her like he did when she was very small. She relaxed against his warmth.

"You know, people said I wasn't Black when I married your mom," Mr. Williams began, as he smoothed his daughter's hair.

Tayesha was shocked. He had never told her that. "Really, Daddy?"

She felt him nodding. "Sure did. They said that I was betraying my race by dating and marrying a White woman. But you know what, pumpkin?"

"What?" Tayesha asked.

"I did what was in my heart. I married the woman I loved. I am Black. Both of my parents are Black, and so are you. Nothing or nobody will ever change that." He smiled at her.

"Tayesha, Black people come in many beautiful shades, and you, baby girl, are a lighter-skinned version of that beauty." He cupped his daughter's face in his hands and looked in her eyes.

"But, Dad, be honest. I don't look Black, do I?"

"Yes you do. You look like other light-skinned Black folks in our race. There are many of them. And remember, color has something to do with being Black, but it's just one piece of the puzzle. God gave you a White mother and a Black father. And we're raising you to embrace and celebrate both sides of your lineage. But yes, you are Black. When you go out into the world, you will be treated as a person of color.

"Most people can look at you, Tayesha and tell you're a light-skinned Black person. And if they can't tell, or aren't sure, that doesn't make you any less Black. Being Black cannot be defined as simply as you would give a definition for a table, or this bed we're sitting on. It's so many wonderful things, not just one or two. You want a definition of Blackness? Being Black has to do with your soul, your ancestry, your culture, not just the amount of melanin you have in your skin. That's the best I can give you honey. But no matter what, don't ever let anybody, or yourself, make you feel less than. That's why I've always told you the importance of learning about our history as a people. Know who you are and, honey, the rest will fall in place. Okay?"

Tayesha smiled and sniffed. "I got it."

"Now about Eddie. It's possible that he's calling to apologize, Tay. Why don't you give him a chance?"

Tayesha thought it over. "I guess I can do that," and she gave her father a big hug.

"Thanks for the talk, Daddy," she said.

"Anytime," he winked and left the room.

* * * * * * *

Later that night, Tayesha brushed her teeth at the sink in the bathroom and thought about the events of the last few days. She tried out for the part of Ashley in the school play and got a callback, thanks to Mrs. Kemp. Then she found out that Mrs. Kemp's student judges were prejudiced and were plotting to keep her out of the leading role. And the worst of all, she had a falling out with Eddie, her good friend of many years.

She had promised her dad that she would talk to Eddie when he called. Maybe she should've said if he called back. Three calls earlier, and now that she had decided to talk to him, the phone was silent. Just as Tayesha decided she wasn't going to sweat it, the phone rang.

Tayesha walked out of her room and halfway down the steps. She had been asking her parents for her own telephone, but so far the answer had been, "Not for another year."

She leaned over the rail to hear. Her father was talking. She turned to go back to her room when her father called.

"Tayesha! Telephone for you. Ten minutes."

Tayesha walked slowly down the steps.

"Ten minutes, Tay," he reminded her, pointing to a clock on the wall that was approaching her bedtime of 10:00 p.m.

"Okay," she mouthed as she took the cordless phone from her dad. She took a deep breath.

"Hello."

"Hey, Tayesha." It was Eddie.

"Hey, Eddie," she said plainly.

"I didn't think you'd take my call. You haven't taken any of the others."

"No, I haven't." Tayesha said defensively, as she walked up the stairs to her room. "Not after what you said to me at Papa's Grill today. How could you say that to me, Eddie?" she asked.

"It was a messed-up thing to say and I'm really, really, sorry, Tayesha. Shoot, I wouldn't have talked to me either." There was silence for several moments and Tayesha wondered if Eddie was still there.

"Hello?" she asked.

"I'm here. Uh…" Eddie began. "I know I've been acting crazy weird lately, it's just that..."

Tayesha sighed.

"I know why you've been acting strange." She opened a drawer and absent mindedly began rummaging through it.

Eddie was surprised. "You, you do?" he stammered.

"Of course I do," Tayesha replied. She closed the drawer and began straightening the pillows on her bed. She knew how tired all of her friends were of hearing about her audition, about how nervous she was, blah, blah, blah, Tayesha thought.

"Wow," Eddie sighed. "How did you find out? I didn't think anyone knew."

Tayesha frowned. Huh? Knew what?

Eddie exhaled. "I didn't think anyone knew that…that, I like you."

"You like me," Tayesha repeated blankly. "You like—" She cut herself off when she realized what she was saying.

Had she heard him correctly?

"Um, what did you just say?" she asked to be sure.

"I said, I really like you," Eddie repeated.

Tayesha couldn't believe it.

"You like me? I don't understand," she said, slowly sitting down on the floor by her bed. "That's why you were acting weird? You aren't sick of hearing about the play?"

"No. What made you think that?" Eddie asked.

"The way you were acting, I thought it was because I was talking about the play too much, and I thought the others were getting sick of hearing about it too, only they weren't showing it..." She stopped when she heard Eddie laughing.

"What's so funny?" Tayesha stood up. She couldn't believe he had the nerve to laugh right now.

Eddie stopped laughing. "This whole thing." He swept his hand through the air as if she could see. "You thought I was mad at you about the play when I was acting strange because I wanted to go out with you, but I was uncomfortable being around you, not to mention nervous about what the others would say or if you would even like me the same way." He caught his breath. "Tayesha, I'm really sorry for hurting your feelings before and in the restaurant today. I just didn't know how to act around you anymore."

"Really," Tayesha said dryly. So he wasn't mad at her. Did he expect her to quickly forgive him and to go out with him? Then another question popped into Tayesha's mind. Why did he like her? She considered her friends. Liz was so talented and outgoing. Naimah was so smart and pulled together. And they were both pretty. Tayesha's head was beginning to hurt again.

"I don't know what to say, Eddie. You really hurt my feelings in the restaurant today."

Awkward silence filled the air. Tayesha pulled at a string on her comforter, an act that her mother would have disapproved of.

Eddie didn't know what to say either. "Well, uh, how do you feel about me? I mean, umm, do you like me, Tayesha? You know, as a boyfriend?"

Silence.

"If you don't feel like that, it's cool with me," Eddie said, trying to be nonchalant. "I'm not going to be mad or anything."

"After what you did to me today, I don't even know if I want you for a friend. I have to go now, Eddie."

"But…" Eddie began.

"I'll talk to you later." And with that, Tayesha hung up and Eddie was left holding the phone.

* CHAPTER EIGHT *

"Does everybody understand their jobs?" Naimah asked as she reached for a can of soda. It was Wednesday after school, and Tayesha, Eddie, Naimah, Liz and Anthony were sitting in Naimah's basement finalizing a plan to deal with Brett and Kaylie.

"Tayesha's callback is Monday, and that'll be here before we know it," Naimah reminded.

Eddie nodded sharply as he spoke. "We're ready." He sneaked a look at Tayesha. She saw him looking at her, and turned her head. Although she was glad Eddie had apologized, Tayesha hadn't yet decided what to do about their friendship. Her feelings were still hurt, and her head was spinning from all the drama she'd found herself in lately. So she thought it would be best if she and Eddie didn't speak for a while so she could be alone with her thoughts.

If the others noticed the awkward exchanges between Eddie and Tayesha, they didn't let on.

"We have a great plan, guys," Tayesha said, careful not to look Eddie's way. "I believe it'll work." She sounded sure and was so grateful to have NEATE by her side.

"It's one thing to be a prejudiced jerk," Naimah said matter-of-factly. "It's another to have the power to put your messed-up views into practice to hurt somebody else. We're going to strip these girls of their power." The others nodded in silent agreement.

"Guys, I want to apologize for being the cause of bad energy between all of us lately." Eddie spoke clearly, but softly. He didn't want to look at his friends until he'd said what he had to say.

"I've been acting really messed up to all of you, but mostly to Tayesha. I just hope she'll accept my apology. What I said to her in the restaurant was terrible and I feel really bad about hurting her feelings. I owe you all an apology."

He looked around the room. His four friends looked at him, not angrily, as Eddie thought they would, but expectantly.

Eddie knew what he was about to do was not going to be easy, but it might be the only way to get through to Tayesha.

"You have been acting a little strangely, Eddie, now that you mention it," Liz commented.

"Yeah," Anthony chimed in. "I just figured it was school stuff."

"No," Eddie began hesitantly. He took a deep breath and stared at the floor.

"I've been, um, stressed out because, um, well, I wanted to ask Tayesha out, but I didn't want her to know or you all to know, 'cause I didn't know how she would take it or how you all would take it, and how it would affect our friendship…"

"Whoa, partner. What'd you just say?" Liz put both hands around her soda can to steady her grip. "You're about to make me drop my soda. You want Tayesha to go out with you?"

"Yeah," Eddie said to the floor. Naimah's jaw dropped. Liz's eyes widened. Anthony just looked confused.

"What do you mean, go out? Where are you going?" Anthony asked.

"Going out as in boyfriend and girlfriend, Anthony," Naimah said impatiently.

Tayesha wanted the floor to open up and swallow her whole. "It wasn't enough to embarrass me once," she said. "You had to do it again?" She couldn't even look at Eddie. "Telling everybody…"

Eddie tore his eyes from the floor and broke into a smile that surprised even him. "So, Miss Tay, whatd'ya say?"

Tayesha smiled in spite of herself. "You really are crazy, Eddie."

"And you like crazy, don't you?" Eddie teased.

"Yeah, I guess I do," Tayesha replied.

"I don't believe any of this," Naimah exclaimed. "Did Eddie just ask Tayesha out and did she just say 'yes?' Is this really happening?"

Liz nodded. "Yep. It's happening, alright."

"So, you all are cool with this, right?" Eddie wanted to know. He sat down next to Tayesha, and grinned at her. She shyly smiled back.

"It doesn't look like it really matters what we think," Liz grinned. "Eddie and Tayesha, sitting in a tree…"

Eddie rolled his eyes good-naturedly. "Awww, cut it out, Liz."

"I will not. You two make a cute couple." Liz said. "Though I admit, this is going to take some getting used to."

Naimah stood and walked over to Eddie and Tayesha. "Well," she said matter-of-factly, smiling at them, "if you two are happy, I think I speak for us all when I say we're happy for you, right Anthony?"

She turned to the chair where Anthony had been sitting. It was empty.

"Anthony?" Naimah called as Liz, Tayesha and Eddie looked around the room for their friend. Suddenly Naimah's basement door slammed shut and the four friends realized that Anthony was on the other side of it.

* * * * * * *

"Here we are, kids." Mrs. Delaney looked in the rearview mirror at her two passengers and smiled. Tayesha stretched as much as the seat belt would allow, and looked over at Eddie. He was grinning at her. She grinned back.

They'd only been going out for a few days, but in that short time, Tayesha and Eddie spent as much time together as their parents allowed. They studied together sometimes, but mostly they talked on the phone. This was the first time the two of them were going somewhere without their friends. A real date, Tayesha thought as she, Mrs. Delaney, and Eddie piled out of the car and stretched in the Saturday afternoon sun. Tayesha smiled at Eddie again. The State Fair was the perfect first date.

At the ticket booth, Eddie proudly pulled out his wallet and bought the State Fair Special, 20 tickets for 15 dollars. Eddie turned a mischievous eye to The Scream, the fair's scariest and most advertised ride. He looked at Tayesha and spoke in his most fear-provoking voice.

"Are you afraid of…The Scream?"

Tayesha looked him dead in the eye. "The question is, are you afraid of The Scream?"

"I'll answer that. Yes," Mrs. Delaney interjected. Tayesha and Eddie laughed.

Eddie looked at his mother disbelievingly. "Come on, Ma. Dad told me that you and he used to get on all the wild roller coaster rides when you were dating."

"Umm-hmm," Mrs. Delaney agreed. "There was no ride too tall, too fast, too wild for your dad and me in those days. No sir. But I don't remember any rides like The Scream back then. What we considered scary, you two would probably consider babyish. The Scream is honestly the scariest looking ride I have ever seen. You two make sure you're buckled up and you hold on tight."

"We will," Tayesha promised with a smile. She welcomed any excuse to cuddle up to Eddie. She craned her neck again to look up at the monster ride.

"Ready?" Tayesha asked Eddie.

"Am I? Come on!" Eddie grabbed her hand. They dashed off to get in line.

"Be back at the car by eight," Mrs. Delaney called after them.

The Scream was worth the three tickets Eddie and Tayesha paid apiece. The two rode on scary roller coasters until they got hungry.

"What do you want to eat?" Eddie asked, his stomach grumbling.

"Let's see." Tayesha's eyes traveled around the area, her senses abuzz with all the wonderful smells and delicious looking foods on display. After some deliberation, Eddie spotted a gyro stand and they ran over to get in line.

"Have you noticed how much time we've spent in line here?" Eddie asked as they bit into their gyros. "Lines for rides, lines for food. We've probably spent an hour of our time here just waiting in line."

Tayesha nodded, her mouth full of food. She put

up a finger, so Eddie would know she had something to say as soon as she swallowed her food.

"Yeah. That's the fair for you. But I really don't mind the lines and the waiting. I've had too much fun today." Her eyes were bright with excitement.

Eddie looked at her. "Me too, Tayesha. Because I'm here with you."

* CHAPTER NINE *

"Well, did you have fun?" Naimah asked excitedly. She looked closely at her friend. "You sure don' t look like someone who went to the fair with her sweetheart." Naimah raised her eyebrows at Tayesha. "You look like you swallowed a lemon!"

"Are you kidding?" Tayesha answered in a hushed voice. "Eddie all but called me a pig!"

Naimah looked at her friend incredulously.

"That's right," Tayesha continued. "We were eating gyros when Eddie"—she practically hissed his man—"started laughing. So naturally, I asked him, "What' s so funny?" I really thought he was thinking of a joke to share with me.

"This brother busts out with, 'Tay, you are handling that sandwich better than any guy I know.' Girl, I was so embarrassed!" Tayesha glared at Eddie. "Said I eat like a guy. That's calling me a pig, I told him. 'I didn't call you a pig,' he said. 'I just said you eat like a guy.' Like he was giving me a compliment!" Tayesha fumed. "Oooh, what did I ever see in him?" she whispered angrily as she sat cross-legged on the worn carpet, giving her account of her and Eddie's fight the previous night.

"Talk about a short-lived romance. You guys were a couple for what, two days?" Liz said in a stage whisper.

"Thank you, Elizabeth," Tayesha emphasized.

"I know you all are whispering about me over there, and that isn't right." Eddie said to the three girls. His brow was furrowed.

"Whatever Tayesha tells you, I did not call her a pig. I would never say that. I know she's telling you about that ridiculous fight we had and the fact that we broke up. She should have kept our business between us, but no." Eddie complained.

"Will you four chill?" Anthony whispered sharply. "Enough of the drama. We don't want to draw attention to ourselves up here. We're in the middle of a meeting, remember?" He splayed both hands out in front of him.

Naimah, Liz, Anthony, Tayesha and Eddie were sitting in a little-used hallway on the third floor of the school. No one but the custodians ever seemed to go up there, so privacy was almost guaranteed. Still the five friends wanted to be careful.

Tayesha looked around. She was relieved the day had finally come, but she was nervous as well.

She had enough on her mind with the play, and wondering whether she and her friends would be able to stop Brett and Kaylie. Then to top it off, she and Eddie had had a stupid fight and broke up. She looked over at Eddie. He all but growled at her. She rolled her eyes and folded her arms across her chest as if she didn't care. Anthony motioned for them to come closer together.

"Okay everybody. Today is the day Operation Expose goes into effect. We all know what's riding on this. And Tayesha's our girl, but we're not going through all this trouble just so Tayesha can get the role she wants."

"You have a way with words, Anthony," Tayesha said, sarcastically, and the others laughed. Anthony wasn't smiling.

"Well it isn't just about you." Anthony mumbled. "It's about exposing and stopping prejudice behavior."

Anthony continued. "We have a lot to do." After a moment, he turned to the others. "Is everybody clear on how this is all going down?"

Everyone nodded uncertainly. The tension was thick in the room. Naimah, the peacemaker, stood.

"United we stand, divided we fall. The last thing we need is to start fighting among ourselves. I know we're all tired and ready   to teach these girls a lesson, but we need to keep cool, everybody. Right?"

The other four nodded.

"Okay, everybody," Naimah continued. "We all know our roles, so let's turn our attention to something else, something that if we let it continue, will foil not only Operation Expose, but also our friendship. Eddie? Tayesha? What's up with you two? One day you're cheesing at each other, doodling each other's name on your notebook, going to the fair, the next, you're fighting and not speaking to each other. You two need to resolve this, this, whatever it is, " Naimah folded her arms across her chest.

"You're right Naimah," Eddie spoke. "Tayesha, I'm really sorry for the fight. I wasn't trying to call you a pig."

"Tayesha?" prompted Naimah.

Tayesha looked at Eddie. "I'm sorry too, Eddie," she muttered.

"You're sorry, he's sorry, we're all sorry," Liz said. "Now that the air has been cleared, can we please wrap this meeting up? I don't know about you all, but I'm ready to teach those two a lesson."

The others voiced their agreement.

"Sounds good to me," Anthony said. "Now, I'll ask again. Does everybody remember what they're supposed to do? It's now or never." Tayesha looked at each of her friends as they answered affirmatively, and she felt a swell of pride.

Naimah looked at Tayesha. "I know just what you're thinking, Tay. I feel it too."

Eddie stood up, looking somber. "Let's do this."

* * * * * * *

For the umpteenth time, Tayesha looked around the girls' locker room. She had a pre-determined hiding place that she was prepared to run to. From that post, Tayesha could see when someone entered the locker room. For the plan to work, she needed two someones to enter the locker room: Brett and Kaylie. If the twin headaches did make an appearance as Tayesha and her friends expected them to, Operation Expose would swing into play.

Tayesha took a deep breath and exhaled. If she let her nerves get the best of her, she could blow the whole thing. No successful plan. No shot at the lead role. And Brett and Kaylie would get away with their foul plan. There was too much at stake.

Tayesha surveyed the scene and went over the plan in her head. Everybody was in place. She was in the locker room. Just outside of the locker room door stood Eddie and Anthony. They pretended to be talking, but were in fact poised to knock on the door and alert Tayesha to Brett or Kaylie's presence.

The plan came together when Tayesha found out that Brett and Kaylie hung out in the drama department locker room after school every day. Tayesha's job was to tape Brett and Kaylie saying something about their plan to keep Tayesha from getting the role of Ashley. After catching them on tape, Tayesha would bring the tape to Mrs. Kemp.

Tayesha sighed anxiously. NEATE's whole plan was built around the possibility of Brett and Kaylie saying something incriminating so Tayesha could catch them on tape and play it for Mrs. Kemp. The five friends hoped that Brett and Kaylie would be dismissed from judging the callbacks and Tayesha, and any other person for that matter, would have a fair chance at the lead role of Ashley. It was Monday, and because the callbacks were on Wednesday, immediately after school, they didn't have much time. This plan had to work today.

Tayesha was a nervous bundle of energy. Just the thought of Brett and Kaylie succeeding in their scheme made her stomach do flips. Tayesha sat on a bench, listening to the steady hum of the water fountain. Every now and then she pressed 'record' on the tape recorder just to make sure it worked.

Knock, knock, knock.

The sound was unmistakable. Eddie and Anthony were telling her that someone was entering the locker room. Tayesha's heart pounded as she scampered over to her hiding place. She crouched down between the wall and the soda machine. She hoped no one got thirsty.

"I talked to Mrs. Kemp today." Tayesha heard a girl's voice say.

"About the play?" Great, Tayesha thought. It must be Brett and Kaylie. She pressed "record" so she wouldn't miss any of their conversation.

"Allison, do you know she gave me a 'D' for a final performance grade?"

Allison? She didn't need an Allison, she needed a Brett and a Kaylie. Tayesha mumbled and pressed "stop." False alarm.

Tayesha settled back into her space. She listened as more people entered the locker room and left. Each time, Tayesha got her hopes up, and each time her hopes were dashed because it wasn't Brett and Kaylie. Tayesha glanced down at her watch. She'd been waiting for nearly an hour. Her knees felt like she had been waiting for four.

"They probably won't even come in here today. This isn't going to work," she whispered bitterly. "How crazy were we—was I—to think we could catch these two on tape. The hours of planning, the high hopes we all had. And my friends did it mainly to help me."

Her vision blurred, and to her annoyance, tears began pouring from her eyes. There she was, pressed between the soda machine and the wall, crying, and she couldn't stop.

"You have an inner strength you don't even know you have, princess," her dad told her once.

"Inner strength my foot," Tayesha muttered bitterly. "Stand up for yourself, princess. Well, I try to stand up for myself and look how it turns out," she sniffed. "And now I'm crying like a big ole baby..."

Busy feeling sorry for herself, Tayesha didn't hear the door open, or the girls talking.

"I have three tests on Thursday," a voice said.

Tayesha wiped her eyes with the back of her hand and strained to listen. For all she knew, it could be two girls named Lucy and Laura. And she hadn't heard Anthony or Eddie knock. She wished she could get a peek at the girls, but she couldn't do that without them seeing her. Shoot.
Tayesha shifted uncomfortably in her spot, trying to steer clear of the wires coming out of the machine. Getting electrocuted was not part of the plan.

The voices were coming closer to Tayesha's hiding

spot. Not good.

"We can, um, study together." The girls neared even closer. Tayesha slid her sweaty palms across her jeans and held her breath.

"Who said anything about studying?" Laughter. "I'll give one of the guys the honor of letting me copy off of their test. When in doubt, look about!"

Tayesha reached for the tape recorder and pressed 'record.' It sounded like Brett and Kaylie, but Tayesha still wasn't sure.

"You've already gotten busted once for cheating. Why don't you just study?"

The girls seemed to have stopped near Tayesha's hiding place. Tayesha bit down on her lip, and let her head rest against the coolness of the soda machine. She leaned as close to the edge of the machine as she dared and again strained to listen. She checked the tape recorder to make sure it was still working. What she heard next made her want to dance on top of the tape recorder.

"Why don't I study? And who are you supposed to be? You have much nerve, Kay. Are you still upset over the play thing? If I'd let you, you'd let that Black girl win the lead role in the play, wouldn't you? I don't care how good she is, Tayesha ain't starring in 'Downside Up Day.'"

Bingo! It was definitely Brett and Kaylie! Tayesha could tell by the arrogant, clipped, tones which one was Brett. The other mousier one would be her yes-girl, Kaylie. Now, if they'd just talk some more about her and the play. Tayesha crossed her fingers so tightly she began to lose circulation.

"I will be soooo glad when these callbacks are over and done with, Kay. Mrs. Kemp seems to really be listening to our recommendations, but anything can happen between now and Wednesday."

Tayesha frowned. She knew she had reason to be worried.

"She keeps talking about Tayesha." It was Kaylie's voice. "She could do even better at callbacks, and then Mrs. Kemp might go ahead and override our recommendations. We're just student judges. Mrs. Kemp can do what she wants."

"I know she can do whatever she wants," Brett whined. Then, her voice brightened. "That's why we have to, should I say, help, things go in the direction we want them to. And, I came up with the perfect plan."

Tayesha checked her recorder to make sure the wheels were still rolling.

"What if Tayesha isn't even there for the callbacks on Wednesday?" Brett said slyly.

Tayesha's ears perked up. Their plan was getting more and more calculated and under-handed. This reminded her of the bathroom conversation she overheard days before. Only this time Tayesha was prepared and in control.

"What do you mean, 'if Tayesha isn't there for the callbacks?'" Kaylie asked. That was exactly what Tayesha wanted to know.

Brett had answers. "This is what we're going to do. Tell me this isn't brilliant. You know, Donna Lewis from our drama class? She's an office assistant. Donna's a sweetie. She'll do whatever I tell her. She is going to page Tayesha so she'll be in the office when she's supposed to be at the callbacks. You know Mrs. Kemp made it clear everyone has to be on time."

Kaylie was quiet for a second. "But how do you know Tayesha'll have a message, Brett?

Brett snorted in disgust. "How slow can you be, Kaylie! Good grief! It won't be a real message. We'll have Tayesha paged so she'll think she has a message. Mop-Top will get a slip telling her to go to the office. Donna will stall to keep her there. By the time that girl gets to the auditions, Mrs. Kemp will tell her 'too late.' Mrs. Kemp believes in fairness and promptness. She isn't going to let one person bend the rules. Our little biracial friend won't even get a chance to audition because she'll be so busy running across campus to answer an 'important message.'" Brett laughed.

"I don't know Brett," Kaylie began. "It seems like a lot of work, and we can get in trouble. Is it really worth it?"

Brett let out an angry sigh. "I said it once, and I'll say it again. Ashley is not going to be a Black person."

Tayesha was stunned, but grateful. She had it all right there on tape.

* * * * * * *

Tayesha waited until she no longer heard Brett's and Kaylie's voices in the large room before she stood to leave her hiding place. She squeezed from between the soda machine and the wall, straightened her back, and stretched. Still reeling from what she had just heard, she stared at the wall, deep in thought.

"How long have you been here?"

Tayesha turned around and came face to face with a wild-eyed Brett. Tayesha didn't know if Brett had seen her leave from her hiding place or what she knew, if anything. Tayesha had been careful to wait until the girls had gone. Obviously, she hadn't been careful enough.

The two girls stared at each other. Brett's face was a mask of anger. The heat of anger that rose in Tayesha surprised her.

"Were you spying on us?"

"I don't answer to you," was Tayesha's curt reply. She tightened her grip on the tape recorder that was tucked underneath her arm.

"You have a tape recorder! D...d...did you tape me?" Brett stuttered.

"You must not have heard me," Tayesha replied calmly, making her way across the locker room to the exit door. "But I'll tell you this. You won't be judging any more auditions." Tayesha watched Brett's expression change from arrogant and angry to apologetic in a matter of seconds.

"You think we don't like Black people, is that it?" Brett asked, trying another tact. "Gosh, I probably would too if I were you. I know what you think you heard, Tayesha," Brett said, faking sincerity. She smiled amicably. "I can explain everything, Tayesha."

"Oh, now I'm Tayesha, huh?" Tayesha shook her head. " I thought I was 'that biracial girl.' I don't need you to explain anything. I have you on tape, Brett." Tayesha looked the girl squarely in the eyes. Brett's anger resurfaced.

"You did tape me!" she hissed. "You taped me and Kaylie without our permission. You can't do that!" she yelled, sending spit flying out of her mouth.

"Too late," Tayesha said smoothly. She walked out of the door, leaving a stunned Brett to stomp around the locker room alone.

Tayesha bumped into Anthony and Eddie on her way out. They pressed her for details.

"Did you get it?" they asked.

"Got it!" Tayesha beamed. "Where is she?" she asked, referring to Mrs. Kemp.

"Upstairs in her office. Naimah and Liz just called."

Tayesha would have to go back the way she came. She turned, and ran back into the locker room. She nearly collided with Brett who was standing angrily in the same place Tayesha had left her. The two made eye contact, then Tayesha took off through the locker room, with Brett on her heels. Tayesha ran through the drama department to the stairs, and headed for Mrs. Kemp's third-floor office.

"Give me that tape!" Brett hollered behind her.

Tayesha kept going, bounding the steps two at a time. Once she made it to the third floor, she paused for a second to catch her breath, then sped down to Mrs. Kemp's door. Brett had just made it to the second flight of stairs when Tayesha balled her fingers into a loose fist and knocked.

"Come in," Mrs. Kemp called out. Tayesha dashed in and closed the door. When she walked in to the drama teacher's office, Tayesha was astonished at what she saw. Kaylie was sitting comfortably in a director's chair.

"Hi Tayesha. Good audition Friday," she said pleasantly. "Congratulations on your callback."

"Thank you," Tayesha answered. "Mrs Kemp, may I speak to you?" Tayesha looked at Kaylie. Kaylie made no move to leave.

"Privately, please?" Tayesha added pointedly.

"Sure," Mrs. Kemp replied. "Kaylie, let me talk to Tayesha. We'll finish talking later." Kaylie tried to smile, but it was clear that she wanted to stay.

"Okay, Mrs. Kemp," Kaylie said as she moved toward the door. "I'll come back—"

Suddenly the office door swung open, nearly hitting Kaylie. A panting, out-of-breath Brett staggered in. The girl looked as if she had run a marathon and was in bad need of hydration. Brett wildly looked around the room and when she spotted the tape recorder, gazed at it longingly. Tayesha moved protectively closer to the tape recorder. Brett slit her eyes at Tayesha. Tayesha gave her a little smile.

"Mrs. Kemp," Brett huffed. "This girl... should be disqualified....from auditioning....for the play." Brett tried to catch her breath as she spoke. Kaylie slunk further into the office and stood against the wall. Like a weasel, Tayesha thought.

Mrs. Kemp was confused and startled at Brett's entrance. She looked at the teen for several moments before responding.

"Brett Mulligan!" she said sharply. "What has gotten into you, barging into my office like this? And what's this business about disqualifying Tayesha? You'd better explain yourself." Mrs. Kemp's eyes bounced between Brett and Tayesha as she waited for an answer.

Tayesha felt adrenaline flowing to every bit of her body, but she worked to retain her cool.

"She does not deserve a callback and she certainly does not deserve to play Ashley. " Brett looked triumphant. Her voice was cold, and halting, like a robot's. It gave Tayesha chills. Brett's voice wasn't that of a thirteen-year-oldgirl.

Mrs. Kemp continued to look from Brett to Tayesha.

"Brett, you've told me absolutely nothing. Tayesha, what do you have to say about all of this? Was this what you wanted to talk to me about?"

Tayesha took the tape recorder from under her arm, put it down and pressed the rewind button. She glanced at Kaylie, who looked like a deer caught in headlights. Then her gaze settled on Brett. Brett's face was balled up in anger. Tayesha pressed play. The beginning of the tape started with a lot of gushing air.

Tayesha began proudly, "It's all right here, Mrs. Kemp. Brett and Kaylie wanted to—"

Before Tayesha could finish her sentence, Brett let out a shriek.

"Give me that tape recorder!" Brett interrupted in a screech, and lunged for the tape recorder.

Tayesha snatched the device out of the girl's reach just in time. She pressed the stop button.

"Brett!" Mrs. Kemp yelled. "Sit down. Now!" She looked at Brett as if she dared her to move. Brett slumped into the chair near the door.

"Tayesha?" Mrs. Kemp motioned toward the tape recorder. Now, all eyes were on her.

This was her moment. Tayesha pressed "play" and waited. To her horror, the machine rumbled and spit out a loud gush of air, and then it went silent. Tayesha felt the room spinning. Her heart stopped beating. Several seconds passed, but still the tape recorder played nothing. Tayesha was sure she had gotten at least some of their conversation on tape. What happened?

Tayesha tried to keep her composure. This was a nightmare. She held her head high, determined not to fall apart in front of Mrs. Kemp and the monster twins. She hit stop, rewound the tape again, and tried the play button one more time. The tape replayed more gushing air, then crackling and shuffling. Mrs. Kemp eyed Tayesha impatiently. Tayesha looked up and caught a glance of Brett's smug face. She would just have to tell Mrs. Kemp, tape or no tape.

Gulping, Tayesha began talking. "It seems something went wrong with my tape." She sighed and willed herself to go on.

"Um, Mrs. Kemp. What I wanted to tell you about is what the tape would have proven. And yes, it does have to do with the play. I was in the right place at the right time, twice. Had I not been, I never would have learned that these two girls, your student judges, Brett Mulligan, and Kaylie O'Donnell," Tayesha made eye contact with them, "have been scheming to keep Black students out of the play. We never had a fair chance. I just can't believe this stupid tape player didn't record their nasty conversation. I don't know what could have happened, Mrs. Kemp," Tayesha managed to add, "but I'm telling you the truth."

Brett seemed to come alive. "What's the matter?

You didn't tape anything after all? Poor baby." She sneered.

"Do you see, Mrs. Kemp. She's such a liar. Telling lies on Kaylie and me…"

The look on Brett's face changed abruptly as the room was suddenly filled with more gushing air and voices. Hers and Kaylie's.

"You've already gotten busted once for cheating," Kaylie's voice sprang from the tape recorder. *"Why don't you just study?"*

"Why don't I study?" Brett's voice answered. *"And who are you supposed to be? You have much nerve, Kay. Are you still upset over the play thing? If I'd let you, you'd let that Black girl win the lead role in the play, wouldn't you? I don't care how good she is, Tayesha ain't starring in 'Downside Up Day.'"*

Tayesha smiled broadly. Watching the sick look on Brett's face and the terrified expression on Kaylie's face as they listened to themselves on tape made Tayesha's and NEATE's hard work worth it. Mrs. Kemp's mouth was a perfect "O".

"We certainly do have a problem here." Mrs. Kemp glared at Brett and Kaylie.

Tayesha breathed a sigh of relief. It was over.

* * * * * * *

"Tayesha Williams."

Tayesha took a deep breath. She walked to the stage and stood there dramatically, ensuring that all eyes in the auditorium were on her. She was ready for this callback. There was no stopping her now. She looked down into the audience and saw Anthony, Liz, Naimah, and Eddie sitting in the front row. Her confidence swelled. She delivered her lines with every ounce of oomph she had, and to her delight, she received a thunderous applause.

Eddie, Anthony, Liz, and Naimah met her outside the auditorium. They jumped up and down, taking turns congratulating her.

"Tay, you were so good!" Liz told her, squeezing her friend.

Tayesha was giddy with excitement. She could not remember ever being this excited about anything. "Girl, thanks! I feel great! I'm pretty good at this acting thing," she beamed patting herself on the shoulder.

"I can't believe you're saying that. It's about time you give yourself some props," Eddie smiled. "You really were good."

"Thanks, Eddie."

"Now we just need to hear from Mrs. Kemp." Naimah announced. "Then, it'll be official."

"She told us it would take about thirty minutes after the callbacks ended before she would come back out and name the final cast," Tayesha told them.

She stood on a bench and looked in the auditorium window. "And they're finished. I was next to last. The girl behind me just finished, everybody!" she whispered breathlessly. Her friends fell silent.

"Can you see Mrs. Kemp?" Naimah wanted to know.

"Yeah. She's sitting on the front row. Most of the kids are waiting in the auditorium for the results. I'm too pumped up. I need to stay out here so I can work off some of this nervous energy." Tayesha exhaled. She turned to face her friends.

"Thanks guys for being here to support me."

"There she goes getting all soft on us," Anthony pretended to be annoyed. But his eyes were smiling.

Tayesha felt as if she were walking on clouds. But an hour later, with no word from Mrs. Kemp, Tayesha began having doubts. Maybe she hadn't gotten the part after all! All five teens were sitting on the bench that Tayesha had stood on to peek in the window.

"I'm getting hungry," Liz complained. "Come on, Mrs. Kemp."

Tayesha was lost in her own thoughts. There were at least a half a dozen girls who got callbacks for the role of Ashley. She hadn't bothered to watch them audition. She was too nervous. Now, she wished she had. At least then she would have a better idea of where she stood.

"You know what guys, why should I think I got the part?" Tayesha asked, sharing her doubt with her friends. "That would mean I was the best out of everyone. Some of those girls have been acting since elementary school. I'm a total novice."

Naimah put her hands on her friend's shoulders and looked her straight in the eyes.

"You know what? You need to start thinking more positively, Tay. I'm tired of you always thinking the worst and being so down on yourself. And what if you don't get the role?" Naimah shrugged her shoulders. "That doesn't say anything about your ability to act, or your worth as a person, does it?"

Tayesha shook her head miserably. " We are all so proud of you, girl, for going after this role," said Naimah.

"And for standing up to Brett and Kaylie," Liz added quietly.

"You could have just given up after hearing them talk about you in the bathroom."

"Could have let them get away with their crazy, prejudiced plot," Eddie said. "So stand strong and proud, Tay. Even if you don't get the role, you're still a winner."

"You guys need to write for after-school specials," Tayesha tried to joke. "But you're right. " She turned in the direction of the auditorium and massaged her temples.

"Let's go in now. Mrs. Kemp should be announcing the results soon if she hasn't already," Tayesha told her friends. "It's been more than an hour."

Mrs. Kemp was walking up on stage as the five teens entered and sat down. An expectant hush fell across the room. Tayesha bit her thumbnail anxiously.

"I know you've been waiting for this moment, students." Mrs. Kemp looked at the clipboard in her hand. "I am proud to announce the cast of Dusable Junior High's production of 'Downside Up Day.'"

It soon became clear that Mrs. Kemp was saving the starring role for last. She named the winner of roles for Ashley's mother and father, best friend Whitney, classmates, teacher Mrs. Fuller, and doctor. Somebody tapped Tayesha's shoulder. She turned around to see Cory Waller from history class.

"You know, you really were good at your auditions, Tayesha. I'll bet you get the starring role."

Tayesha smiled, pleasantly surprised. "Thanks,

Cory."

She turned her attention back to Mrs. Kemp.

"I can't stand the suspense!" she exclaimed to Liz who was sitting on her right. Naimah was on her left, Eddie sat next to Naimah, and Anthony sat next to Liz. Tayesha stopped biting her thumbnail and began chewing all her nails.

"Tayesha, you are driving me crazy! Leave your nails alone," Liz whispered.

"Can I bite yours then?" Tayesha asked innocently.

Liz playfully thumped her. "This play is making you lose your mind."

"I think it's already gone," Tayesha said biting her lip. Liz and Naimah gave her a look.

Mrs. Kemp paused. "And last but not least, I am pleased to announce the winner of the role of Ashley," she beamed.

Tayesha grabbed Naimah and Liz's hands instinctively.

"Tayesha Williams, you are Ashley!" Suddenly, there was a groundswell of applause and kids were hugging Tayesha.

"Congratulations, cast!" Mrs. Kemp said. "Rehearsals begin in one week!"

* CHAPTER TEN *

The auditorium at DuSable Junior High School was filled to capacity. It was the opening night of "Downside Up Day." The cast and crew, composed largely of seventh and eighth-grade students, were excited and nervous. The long-awaited evening was here. For the weeks leading up to the play, the school was abuzz with anticipation. Tayesha was beside herself with excitement. She was also beside the toilet in the locker room, throwing up.

"Tonight is your night, Tay. You can't get sick now," Liz called through the bathroom door, as she wet paper towels in the sink."

"I'm going to be fine," Tayesha insisted. But her constant dry heaving was telling a different story.

"We need to get her mom and Mrs. Kemp," Naimah said rubbing Tayesha's back. "No way is she going to be up to performing tonight."

"Yes, I am," Tayesha insisted, holding up her head to look at her friend. "I've worked too hard to get here and I am not missing out because of a little headache." Tayesha stood and crossed her arms across her chest. "Or stomachache," she added weakly.

Naimah stared at Tayesha.

"How do I look?"

"Tay. You look awful." Liz said truthfully as she held a wet paper towel on her friend's forehead. Naimah made a face at her. Liz made one back at Naimah.

"Well, she asked," Liz protested.

Tayesha faked a smile. "Thanks." Then she raised her voice a notch. "Go get my mom!"

Naimah jumped up. "Don't move a muscle. I'll go find her."

"Now where do you thinks she's gonna go, sick as she is, Naimah?" Liz wanted to know.

"On stage," Tayesha whispered hoarsely. "That's where. I'm…going…to…be…alright. Ugh. I have to puke."

"It's time, Tayesha." Mrs. Kemp entered the locker room. Mrs. Williams and Naimah were right behind her. Mrs. Williams rushed over to her daughter. "Baby, are you okay?" Mrs. Kemp looked at Mrs. Williams quizzically.

"Her friend had to come get me, Mrs. Kemp," Mrs. Williams explained. "She told me Tayesha was vomiting." Mrs. Williams's hand instinctively went to her daughter's forehead. "Tayesha? What's wrong?"

"I'm feeling a lot better, Ma," Tayesha offered. "For about twenty minutes up until just now, I was vomiting and my stomach was all cramped up. I think it was just nerves though," Tayesha said weakly.

"Well, how do you feel now? You sound weak." Mrs. Kemp was concerned.

"I'm okay, now." Tayesha moved to walk across the room to sit on a bench.

"Tay, honey," Mrs. Williams said gently. "I know you think you feel better now, but I don't know that you need to perform tonight. As badly as you felt."

Tayesha made it to the bench and sat down. "No, Ma," she said, sounding more like herself. "I can say my lines alright. I've worked too hard for this role to just go home because of butterflies."

"What you had wasn't butterflies. You had geese," Liz added. Tayesha and Naimah looked at Liz and sucked their teeth.

"I think I can make it, Mrs. Kemp," Tayesha said. "As long as Liz doesn't crack any more jokes. I think I can."

"Just like the little engine that could, huh, Tay?" Liz teased. "I think I can, I think I can…"

"Make her stop, please?" Tayesha laughed

weakly. "I'm trying not to laugh here, and you're not helping."

"She's acting silly with her friends. That's a good sign." Mrs. Williams observed with a smile. "But I don't want you getting up on the stage and passing out, Tayesha," her mother said worriedly.

"Sure, you think you feel stronger now, but honey, you don't know how you're gonna feel once you're out on the stage, performing under all those hot lights..."

"And that's my concern as well, Mrs. Williams," Mrs. Kemp said, nodding in agreement.

"Of course, we all want to do the show, but I'm concerned about your well-being, Tayesha. If you're sick, you need to rest and get better before trying to perform. That's why we have understudies. Monica has been studying your part and will be able to take your place. You can rest up tonight so you'll be able to perform tomorrow."

Tayesha looked at her mother, her two best girlfriends, and her drama teacher and made her decision.

Some other girl in her place?

"Oh, no," Tayesha said determinedly. She'd worked too hard to miss her first opening night. Tayesha looked at her mother, and pleaded. "If you'll let me, Ma, I want to perform. Tonight is opening night. The show must go on!"

* * * * * * *

"Where am I?"

"Honey, you must have passed out. You screamed for me, and I heard a thud. When I got to you, you were lying on the floor. How do you feel?"

"I'm fine. But may I ask you something?"

"Sure, honey. Anything."

"Who... are... you?"

Everyone in the audience was focused on the actors on stage.

"Who am I? You didn't fall that hard, did you?" There was a pause. "Um, honey, why are you looking at me like that?"

"Ma'am? Uh, I really mean it. I don't know who you are."

"What's happened to you, Ashley? I'm your mother!"

Tayesha made it through the night with flying colors. When the cast came back out at the play's end, she received a standing ovation.

"Brava!" Mr. Williams said as he and Mrs. Williams walked back stage. "Tayesha honey, you were great." He presented his daughter with a rose. He and Mrs. Williams hugged their daughter.

"You were super, sweetheart," Mrs. Williams gushed.

Liz, Naimah, Eddie, and Anthony approached their actress friend, giving hugs and high fives.

"Sistergirl, that was a slammin' performance!" Liz exclaimed. "Nobody would ever have guessed you had been sick right before going on stage. You looked great."

Eddie started to give her a handshake, but gave her a hug instead. "Good job, Tay. Good job."

Tayesha smiled. "Thanks." Someone tapped her on her shoulder and Tayesha turned around. It was Michelle. The other teens and Michelle recognized each other from school and exchanged greetings.

"You were fantastic, Tayesha!" She gave Tayesha a hug then looked at Eddie, Naimah, Liz, and Anthony. "Everybody heard about what you five did. That's all kids are talking about. And then you," she pointed at Tayesha, "went and brought the house down with that great performance."

Michelle's eyes were bright. Tayesha shared her excitement. The evening had turned out more beautifully than she could have ever hoped for.

"I thought you should have gotten a part," Tayesha told her. "You would have been great yourself."

"That's okay." Michelle waved her hand. "There were others better than I was. What you guys did will help make it so everyone at least gets a fair audition from now on."

After Michelle left, Tayesha turned to her family and friends. "Thanks everybody for everything," she said, full of emotion. "I am trying really hard not to cry."

"You deserve this night, Tayesha. Good performance." Tayesha turned to see who was talking to her. It was Kaylie.

"You have nerve," Liz said angrily, looking directly at Kaylie. "Of all people."

"You and Brett came this close to keeping this 'good performance' from happening, Kaylie," Naimah said coolly. "I can't believe you would even show your face here," she said scornfully.

"What do you want, Kaylie?" Tayesha asked. Her face didn't have a trace of a smile and she stood with her arms crossed in front of her chest.

Kaylie shifted from one foot to the other. "Look, Tayesha. I just want to say I'm sorry for what we did. I was wrong for going along with Brett and trying to keep you from getting the role you wanted. And deserved. You don't have to believe me, and I don't blame you if you don't," Kaylie explained.

"I tried to get Brett to come. She said she wouldn't step foot in here." Kaylie looked uncomfortable.

"But, anyway, you really did a fantastic job. Um, and just to let you know, Mrs. Kemp told us we can't serve as student judges for any more plays, and we were kicked out of the drama department."

Tayesha accepted this bit of information with a sliver of satisfaction. She knew Brett to be the true impetus behind their evil, but Kaylie would not get any slack from her. Tayesha thought about what her father said about people who allow injustice to happen, even though they have the power to stop it. Kaylie was no innocent bystander. Maybe she didn't plot like Brett, but Kaylie stood with her friend in the whole sordid mess, and Tayesha had no love for either of them.

"I appreciate the apology, Kaylie," she said flatly. "Excuse me." Tayesha turned away from Kaylie to talk to her friends. Her parents and her friends' parents were discussing getting together for a dinner celebration at a nearby restaurant. Somebody cleared his throat.

"What can I say?" Anthony smiled self-consciously. "You truly were the b-o-m-b, BOMB!" he exclaimed.

Tayesha laughed. "Silly. Thanks, Anthony," she smiled.

"Uh, I owe you an apology, Tay, Anthony began, "because…"

Tayesha waited patiently.

"You probably guessed it, maybe not. Well, I guess it bothered me that you liked Eddie, 'cause I liked you, too." He looked down and then up at her.

Tayesha caught Anthony's awkward gaze and returned it with an awkward look of her own. So that's why he had been tripping that day at the last planning meeting.

Anthony dropped his head and concentrated on his feet.

"Anthony?" Tayesha began. "I, I…" she trailed off. She didn't know what to say. First Eddie, and now Anthony. She waited for Anthony to say something else. But he was still looking down at his feet.

"Ahhhhhhhhh," Anthony yelled suddenly. He raised his head and threw it back in laughter. "I'm kidding! Look at you, thinking you had another crush." He wiped his eyes.

"You're not the only actor in the group," he chuckled. Tayesha couldn't help but laugh.

"I accept your apology, if you can call it that," she said.

"I wasn't joking about that part," Anthony said. "I was acting crazy. Guess I just didn't like that my best guy friend and one of my best girl friends had something that I wasn't a part of. But I'm over it."

"Good," Tayesha said with a nod. Maybe they could all pick up where they had left off. Just being five really tight friends.

"Uh, can we take this party to the restaurant?" Eddie interrupted. "I'm ready to eat!"

"I'll second that, man. I haven't eaten in hours and I am ready!" Anthony rubbed his stomach.

"So what else is new?" Mr. Delaney said wryly and the entire circle laughed.

"Downside Up Day" was a roaring success. Each night it played, the auditorium was packed to capacity. Naimah, Eddie, Anthony, Tayesha, and Liz had passed out fliers to publicize the play, and hundreds of people from the community came out to see the performance. It didn't hurt that the five had also drummed up even more interest in the play by getting the word out about Brett and Kaylie's scheme. Many kids knew Tayesha as the shy girl" and were interested in seeing her in the spotlight. They weren't disappointed. Tayesha was believable and talented in the starring role as Ashley.

On the final night, Tayesha looked at her friends and family and smiled. Her grandma was right. Sometimes we are tested to find out what we're made of, she thought. And after all of this drama, she knew she was made of some really tough stuff. Tayesha grinned. She now knew she could conquer any test that came her way. Any test at all.

About the Author

Tara Demps Soyinka

"I knew at a young age that writing would figure largley into my personal and professional lives," says Tara Soyinka. Growing up in St. Petersburg, Florida, young Tara spent much of her time reading, writing and participating in oratorical contests. So it was no surprise when she selected English as her major at Florida A & M University. As a Ronald E. McNair Post-Baccalaureate fellow, she conducted a study on the self-concept of first grade African-American children. A kindergarten teacher, and first-time published children's author, today Tara is in a unique position to help shape children's self-images—inside the classroom and beyond. The mother of two says, "I am inspired by my children and all children of African descent to write enjoyable and quality literature that offers them a positive reflection of themselves. "

Tara lives with her husband and children in Atlanta, Georgia.